AGENT Amelia

Spooky Ballet!

Spooky
Ballet!

MICHAEL BROAD

Andersen Press
London

First published
in 2009 by
Andersen Press Limited,
20 Vauxhall Bridge Road,
London SW1V 2SA
www.andersenpress.co.uk
www.michaelbroad.co.uk

Reprinted 2009

Copyright
© Michael Broad, 2009
All rights reserved.
British Library Cataloguing in
Publication Data available.
ISBN 978 1 84270 817 0

Printed and bound in Great Britain
by CPI Cox and Wyman Ltd,
Reading, Berkshire

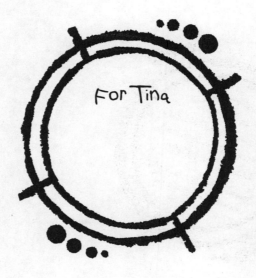

For Tina

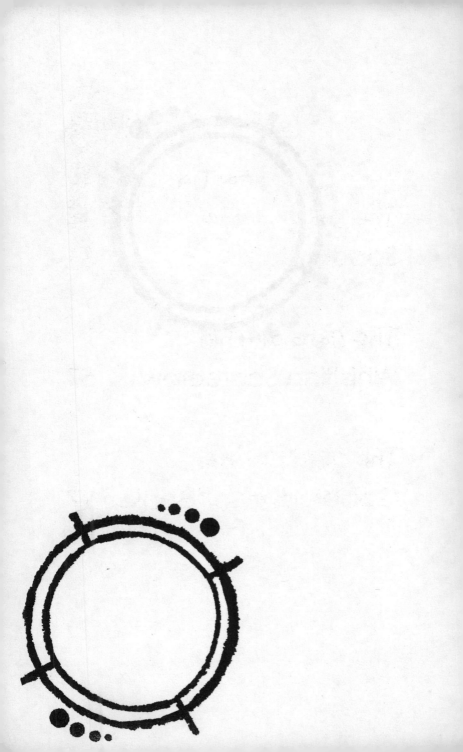

The Case of the
Spooky Ballet   11

The Case of the
Whistling Scarecrow   57

The Case of the
Gobbledygook Books 97

I'M AMELIA KIDD and I'm a secret agent.

Well, I'm not actually a secret agent. I don't work for the government or anything, but I've saved the world loads of times from evil geniuses and criminal masterminds. There are loads of them around if you know what to look for.

I'm really good at disguises. I make my own gadgets (which sometimes work), and I'm used to improvising in sticky situations – which you have to do all the time when you're a secret agent.

These are my Secret Agent Case Files.

The Case of the Spooky Ballet

When you're a secret agent it's always a good idea to have some martial art skills, because evil geniuses and criminal masterminds can turn pretty nasty when you foil their plans to take over the world.

The local village hall advertised loads of different classes in Karate and Jujutsu, and after a week of my dropping hints all over the place, Mum eventually signed me up for an evening class!

Although, she was very vague about exactly *which* martial art I would be studying . . .

When we drove up to the hall there were already a few girls waiting around outside. I thought it was really cool that so many girls had signed up for martial arts, but I did expect to see *some* boys.

'I'll pick you up here in two hours,' Mum said cheerily, as I got out of the car.

'But you still haven't told me which . . . ' I didn't get to finish what I was saying because Mum  waved enthusiastically and sped away, and I couldn't help noticing that she was grinning from ear to ear.

'Hmmm?' I thought, pulling on my rucksack and heading for the hall.

The group of girls were gathered around outside the doors and I froze on the spot when I heard a familiar voice coming from the middle of the huddle.

It was loud and shrill and seemed to
be demanding something.

'Of course she'll pick me!' it
shrieked. 'You lot are like clumsy
hippopotami!'

As the girls backed away I saw
Trudy Hart at the centre! Trudy is my
arch nemesis at school. She's not an
evil genius or a criminal mastermind,

but she is very spoiled and used to
getting her own way!

When Trudy saw me coming
towards them she abandoned
whatever she was yelling about and
barged past the other girls. She strode
up to me and poked me with her
pointing finger.

'What are *you* doing here?'
Trudy demanded.

'I'm here for the class, of course,'
I said calmly.

'You're training
with Madam Giselle?'
Trudy chuckled.
'Well, this I
have to see!'

I was
about to ask
who Madam
Giselle was when
the doors to the
hall suddenly
burst open, and
standing in the
doorway was a
crooked old woman
with a long black
cane.

'Enter!' she roared dramatically, and then scuttled back into the hall.

Trudy hurried forward to get inside before anyone else, while I tagged along behind. Madam Giselle was obviously the class teacher, but I really couldn't see her delivering a decent karate kick!

Inside the hall everyone started getting changed and as the girls put up their hair, pulled on their tutus and tied the ribbons on their satin shoes, everything suddenly became clear.

My mum is *always* trying to make me do girly things like flower arranging or embroidery,

because she doesn't know I'm a secret agent off saving the world all the time. Now she'd actually *tricked me* into taking ballet lessons!

Seeing the girls fluffing out their identical pink tutus, it occurred to me that there was still a way out. I couldn't be a ballerina in combat trousers and trainers, so I quickly approached Madam Giselle.

'Er, I don't have a tutu or ballet shoes,' I sighed, pretending to look disappointed.

'You must be Amelia Kidd?' sniffed Madam Giselle, eyeing me up and down.

I nodded and tried to ignore Trudy making faces behind the old woman's back.

'I told your mother that all my dancers wear my own *specially designed* tutus and ballet shoes!' said

Madam Giselle, jabbing her cane at a mass of pink frills hanging on the wall behind her. 'And *those* are yours!'

'Great!' I sighed, taking down the dress.

The other girls were chatting while I got changed and I soon discovered that as well as being in the wrong class, I was also several weeks behind. The girls were already dancing *Swan Lake* and apparently, Madam Giselle was about to select the prima ballerina.

' . . . and I'm also the most beautiful!' declared Trudy Hart, having just listed all the reasons why she, and no one else, was qualified for prima ballerina status. 'So there will be big trouble if Madam Giselle doesn't pick me!'

With everyone changed,
Madam Giselle scuttled to the centre
of the hall and tapped her black cane
twice on the wooden floor.

TAP! TAP!

With this, all the girls fluttered
forward and stood in a line on tippy toes.

I sloughed forward feeling miserable and weighed down by frills.

Tugging at the tutu, I couldn't help wondering why it was so heavy for something so frilly. I thought perhaps the 'special design' included weights in the waistband, as it was also pretty lumpy, and I was about to complain when Madam Giselle spoke.

'The prima ballerina is the star of the show!' she said, with a faraway look in her eyes. 'I was once the prima ballerina at the King's Theatre, until I was cut down in my prime! When I turned a mere *seventy*, they told me I was too old . . . '

'Oh, get on with it!' growled Trudy.

Madam Giselle narrowed her eyes at Trudy and then waved the rest of the story away with an elegant swoosh of the hand.

She smiled unconvincingly and then produced a large white tutu. It was twice the width and frilliness of the pink ones we were wearing and had two lengths of ribbon hanging down the sides.

Madam Giselle hobbled along the line of dancers, each girl sighing heavily as the tutu passed them by, and when it eventually stopped at Trudy it seemed to take all her effort not to snatch it from the old woman's hands.

'Trudy Hart,' said
Madam Giselle.
'You will be our
star!'
In a blur
of movement
Trudy ripped
off the pink
tutu, tossed
it over her
shoulder and
wrapped the
crisp white
lace around her
waist. She seemed to sag slightly
as though this tutu was even heavier
than the pink ones, but managed to
keep her head high enough to look
down on the rest of us.

'Now we have much work
to do!' snapped Madam Giselle,
returning to the centre of the hall.
'So you must listen very carefully
– exactly as we rehearsed!' she added,
lifting the cane and tapping it on the
floor again.

TAP! TAP
TAP! TAP!
TAP!
TAP! TAP!

Being a secret agent I've studied
Morse Code – which is an old
fashioned alphabet of dots and dashes
for tapping out messages, and this tap,
tap, tapping sounded very similar.

With every sequence of taps the girls
moved in perfect time with each
other, spinning on their tippy toes and
springing up and down with peculiar
arm movements.

Madam Giselle nodded with
satisfaction at each girl in turn and
then frowned when she got to me.

'Listen to the cane!' she demanded, indicating that I should step in time with the TAP! TAP! TAP! 'Surrender to the tap, tap, tapping!' she whispered.

It was at this point that I suspected something dodgy was going on. Usually I'm pretty quick to spot a criminal genius or a criminal mastermind, but I'd been so horrified

to find myself enrolled in ballet class
I'd ignored all the signs!

The 'specially designed' tutus!
The bitter ballet story!
The Morse Code cane!

I made a point of not
surrendering to the tapping cane and
watched the hand movements of the
other dancers instead. It was then that
I realised these were not graceful ballet
moves at all — they were complicated
mimes that looked like the grabbing
claws of a junkyard crane!

With Madam Giselle
standing next to me I got a good
look at the cane and for the first
time I noticed a small red button
in the silver knob at the top.

Uh Oh!

Red buttons
are very popular with
those attempting to
take over the world.
I've come up against
a few in my time and every one
made *something* explode. I wasn't sure
what would explode if this button
was pressed, so I decided to play along
while I worked it all out.

The looks on the faces
of the other girls seemed
more vacant than usual,
as though the tapping
cane had taken over
their brains.

So I slowly adjusted my expression to look as gormless as the rest of them and tried my best to copy their moves.

It was really hard work spinning and bobbing and grabbing at the same time, but I finally managed to convince Madam Giselle that I was a brainwashed ballerina. She stepped away from me looking very pleased with herself and adjusted the rhythm of taps.

TAP! TAP! TAP! TAP! TAP!
TAP! TAP! TAP! TAP!
TAP! TAP!
TAP! TAP! TAP! TAP! TAP!

There seemed to be twice as many instructions as the cane jabbed at the floor like a sewing-machine needle! Suddenly Trudy leapt away with a series of impressive jumps and spins, followed by the next girl and the next, until it was my turn to do the same.

Fortunately, Madam Giselle was no longer focusing just on me, so she didn't notice that my jumps and spins were not quite so graceful.

The ballerina train snaked around the hall acting out mimes along the way while the teacher watched intently. She spent most of her time watching Trudy the prima ballerina, who had no idea that she was starring in something dodgy and possibly explosive.

Once satisfied that all the dancers would respond to every instruction, Madam Giselle eventually brought the tap tempo down and herded everyone back into a line. Then she paused and made three rapid taps that obviously meant 'stop'.

I was glad for the chance to rest because the dancing was really hard work and I ached all over. A quick glance sideways confirmed that the other girls were still in a trance, which meant I couldn't collapse into an exhausted heap!

'I think it is time for you all to wear your special ballet hats!' said Madam Giselle, mostly to herself as the spooky ballerinas stared straight ahead. She produced a cloth sack and handed something dark and woolly to each of the dancers.

We all pulled on the headgear to reveal the special 'ballet hat' was actually a knitted balaclava!

Beneath the wool my vacant
expression turned to one of shock
as I realised that hiding our faces
meant we were leaving the hall,
and whatever Madam Giselle was
planning was being put into action!

The old teacher scuttled up
and down checking shoe ribbons
and straightening tutus, and then
she pulled on her own balaclava and
leapt on Trudy's back! The ribbons on
Trudy's dress turned out to be stirrups

because the old woman slipped her
pointy black shoes through them.

Perched on Trudy's back, Madam Giselle tugged on her cane extending it to twice its length and began tapping out new instructions that sent Trudy leaping through the doors of the hall, immediately followed by the rest of the dancers.

It was hard work keeping up as the line of ballerinas bounded down the High Street like frilly gazelles, while avoiding startled shoppers who had to dive out of our way. A few onlookers actually applauded as we passed, thinking this was some strange kind of street theatre.

With a few well-timed spins I managed to twirl myself to the front of the regular dancers so I could keep an eye on Trudy and her ridiculous rider, who was holding on with one hand and tapping the cane with the other.

Madame Giselle looked like a crazed crow perched on a wedding cake!

I still had no idea what the demented dancer was planning, or where we were going, when I caught a glimpse of a poster stuck to a lamppost advertising *Swan Lake*!

This was a bit too much of a coincidence, so with sideways leap I snatched it.

TONIGHT!
KINGS
THEATRE
SWAN LAKE

Apparently a new production
of *Swan Lake* was opening that night
at the King's Theatre, which meant
Madam Giselle was herding us
straight for the people she blamed for
the ending of her career!

Suddenly the old woman steered Trudy down an alleyway at the side of the theatre and opened the stage door with a rusty old key. Madame Giselle ushered us inside where the Swan Lake music was already playing, and made her frilly white filly gallop towards the stage!

Uh Oh!

I managed to stay close behind and focused on the cane, knowing I had to nab it before the old woman pressed the red button. I got really close as they neared the wooden platform, but when I grabbed for it Trudy did a massive leap like a prize show-jumper and the next thing I knew we were all on stage!

The audience gasped when
the balaclava ballerinas appeared out
of nowhere and the *real* ballerina
misjudged a jump and landed on
her bottom! Madam Giselle quickly
dismounted Trudy and hobbled to the
front of the stage!

'I have danced my whole life for you ungrateful people!' she roared, snapping her cane back to its regular size and waving it at the stunned audience. 'And now you will all pay!'

I charged to the front of the stage as the old woman lifted the cane to eye level, her crooked thumb hovering over the silver knob.

But just as I went to snatch it she pressed the red button!

Luckily nothing exploded. Instead, the theatre was filled with a whirring sound and when I looked down I saw my tutu beginning to rotate! I quickly grabbed at the spinning frills and after a bit of wrestling it ground to a halt and the motor in the waistband went

'POP!'

Looking around I noticed all
the other tutus were now at full speed
as Madam Giselle tapped out new
instructions that sent the ballerinas
into the audience. The spinning skirts
allowed the girls to leap from seat to
seat and hover above the
crowd as they picked
their pockets and stole
their jewellery.

'Money!' I
gasped. 'You want
them to "pay"
with money?'

For the
first time
Madam Giselle
noticed that
one of her
ballerinas
was standing
behind her not doing as she was told.
She tapped even more frantically with
the cane, but I just folded my arms
and frowned.

'So you're just a common
old thief?' I said, feeling a bit
disappointed that she'd gone to such
insane effort just to rob people.

'You're not trying to take over the
world with an army of brainwashed
ballerinas?'

'Take over the world?' said the
old woman, scratching her woolly
chin. 'No, of course not. But now
you come to mention it, I could easily
modify the cane controls and gather
more girls . . . '

'Oh, give me that!' I snapped, snatching the cane and tapping it three times.

The ballerinas immediately stopped plundering the audience and dropped all the loot. But they were still hovering in the air and looking pretty spooky, like frilly pink ghosts in black balaclavas!

I pressed the red button, which turned off the motors and lowered the dancers to the floor. And it was just in time too, because that was when I heard the police sirens wailing down the High Street.

When you're a secret agent you can't take credit for saving the world – or for saving a theatre full of people from being robbed by a madwoman. You also have to protect the innocent, so I tapped the cane to bring the ballerinas back to the stage.

The tapping instructions were *very* similar to Morse Code, so I extended the cane and hopped onto Trudy's back for the getaway – *only* because I couldn't tap and run at the same time, of course.

Madam Giselle shook her fists
at me as we bounded away, but she
couldn't move without the cane
and had to stay in the limelight
until the police arrested her.

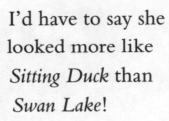

I'd have to say she looked more like *Sitting Duck* than *Swan Lake*!

Back at the hall I removed all the balaclavas and broke the cane in half, which snapped the weary dancers out of their trance. Luckily they remembered nothing of their excursion and were all too exhausted

to care when I told them Madam
Giselle wouldn't be continuing the
class. Well, all but
one . . .

'But I'm the prima ballerina!'
Trudy squealed. 'The star of the
show!'

'The star of the
showjumping more
like,' I chuckled,
and headed for
the door.

Mum was pretty sheepish when I returned to the car, but I didn't give her a hard time about tricking me. Because not only had I *sort of* saved the world again, I'd also learned some brilliant leaps and twirls that would definitely come in handy on secret agent missions.

The Case of the Whistling Scarecrow!

On sunny days, Mum sometimes packs a picnic and drives us out to the country. We find a nice quiet meadow away from the road, lay a blanket under a tree and then laze around all day long. Mum enjoys getting away from the hustle and bustle, and I enjoy getting away from evil geniuses and criminal masterminds trying to take over the world.

Having spotted a suitably idyllic meadow, we unpacked the car and made our way down a winding country lane with the picnic hamper and blanket. I also had my trusty rucksack, because a secret agent has to be prepared for anything.

Which was just as well . . .

As we climbed over the stile into the meadow there was another family coming towards us with a picnic hamper and blankets, but instead of looking happy and relaxed – they looked panic-stricken.

'LEAVE THIS PLACE!' the mother warned, flapping her arms dramatically.

'Excuse me?' Mum gasped, as they bustled past.

'The phantom picnic-nicker has struck!' she said, quickly clambering over the stile, followed by the rest of her family. 'We packed a delicious picnic with sandwiches and cake and apple pie, and now we have nothing!'

I was about to quiz them on the specifics of the buffet burglary, but they were gone before I had a chance – running down the road as fast as their legs would carry them.

It was then that I saw a notice nailed to the stile post.

BEWARE
OF THE PHANTOM
PICNIC-NICKER!
Any food brought
into this meadow
is likely to
mysteriously
vanish!

I snatched the piece of paper before Mum saw it and stuffed it in my pocket.

Even though I was supposed to be having a day off, it was my duty as a secret agent to investigate the mystery.

But first I had to convince Mum that this was still the perfect spot for a picnic.

'How rude!' I said. 'That family *obviously* want the whole place to themselves!'

'What do you mean?' Mum gasped, looking completely bewildered.

'They must have seen us coming down the lane with our picnic basket!' I said, pretending to sound shocked and appalled. 'So they made up that silly story about a phantom to scare us off!'

'But they've left,' Mum frowned, as the fleeing family disappeared around the corner.

'That's just what they *want* us to think,' I said, tipping my sunglasses. 'They're probably hiding behind a bush until we leave and then they'll come back again. Well, we'll show them!' I added, heading straight for the tree in the middle of the meadow.

I'm not sure Mum was *entirely* convinced by my story – but the

alternative was to admit that she
believed in the phantom picnic-
nicker! So she reluctantly followed me
into the field.

Once we'd laid out the blanket
and had a glass of orange squash,
Mum seemed to forget all about
the other family and their bizarre
warning. The spot we'd chosen was
so bright and pretty it looked like the
most innocent place in the world.

When Mum
took out her book and
began reading, it was
time for me to go
to work. I scanned
the hilly meadow
for any likely hiding
places like trees and
hedges, where a food thief might
conceal himself, but the area was
completely open. Then I turned my
attention to the neighbouring crop
fields and narrowed my eyes at the
scarecrows scattered
along the edge.

'I think I'll go and pick some wild flowers,' I said whimsically, grabbing an extra pointy pencil from my rucksack. I took some paper too so it would look like I intended to do some drawing, but I had other plans for the pencil . . .

'OK, darling,' Mum said, peering over her book. 'But stay where I can see you.'

'I will,' I said, and casually made my way towards the nearest crop field.

Skipping along the fence at the edge of the field I paused at each scarecrow and gave it a quick jab in the leg with the pencil, to make sure no one was hiding inside. But none of them flinched.

Then I glanced at the far field and saw a lone scarecrow that was very different from all the others. This scarecrow was different because it was covered in big black crows!

The birds were perched along its raggedy arms and their heads were tilted as though they were listening to something. Then the scarecrow suddenly nodded its head and the crows all took to the sky!

Uh Oh!

The birds hadn't flown very high when they turned in midair and dive-bombed straight into the long grass of the meadow! The crows had vanished, but I could still see their tracks as they beat a path through the grass.

They were heading for our picnic basket!

I legged it across the meadow, hoping to head off the tracks of ruffled grass as the crows charged towards the tree. It was neck and neck as we both drew closer, then I leapt forward and landed at the edge of the blanket. I'd blocked the crows' path and they had no choice but to take to the sky again, shooting out of the grass like feathered rockets.

CAW!
CAW!
CAW!

They went, flapping away angrily.

I turned to make sure Mum was OK
and was relieved to find her fast asleep
with the book flat on her face. Then
I marched down the hill towards
the dodgy scarecrow with the angry
crows now circling above it.

The scarecrow didn't move when I approached, in fact it looked as innocent as all the others. But I'd already seen it nodding  and knew there was *someone* lurking inside, so I pulled out my pencil.

I don't jab people with pointy things if I can help it, so I thought I'd give the crook a chance to surrender.

'Give yourself up!' I said, waving the pencil at him.

Nothing.

'It's very pointy!' I added, tapping the nib with the tip of my finger.

Nothing.

'Well, don't say I didn't warn you!' I said, and jabbed the scarecrow in the leg.

I immediately jumped back, expecting the scarecrow to yelp or yell or jump down and chase me across the field. But like all the other scarecrows, it didn't even flinch. I stepped forward again and gave his brown trousers a few more jabs just to be sure.

Nothing.

When I got no response I grabbed the legs and gave them a prod and a squeeze to discover they were just a pair of old trousers stuffed full of straw. Then I poked its belly and found that it was full of straw too. Finally, I reached up to find that it had saggy straw arms and twigs for fingers.

It was obvious this was just a regular scarecrow, and I decided that the wind must have blown its sack head forward, which scared the crows away and make it *look* like a nod . . .

'Have you quite finished prodding me?' said the scarecrow, tilting its head to peer down at me through two button eyes! 'Because harassing a scarecrow is very rude, you know.'

'ARRRGH!'

I yelled, and darted back a few steps.

'And now you're screaming at me,' sighed the scarecrow, shaking its head from side to side with disapproval. Then it glanced up into the sky at the circling crows and whistled a command. Suddenly the crows all started dive-bombing again, and this time they were heading straight for me!

So I legged it across the field towards the other scarecrows, thinking the birds might actually be scared of these ones. But as I got nearer they didn't seem bothered at all.

I ripped down the nearest scarecrow and pulled on its tatty hat and straw-filled jumper. And I did it just in time because one of the crows pecked my arm with its beak.

The other
birds
swooped down
and pecked
at me too,
but the hat
and stuffed
jumper protected
me from their jabbing beaks. Then, I
flapped my arms around like a lunatic
until the startled birds flew off.

'PHEW!' I sighed, scratching
my itchy head through the hat.

The scarecrow obviously
thought it was clever, using the birds
to pay me back for prodding him
with the pencil, but there was still
one thing about all this that just didn't
make sense.

SCARECROWS CAN'T TALK!

I've seen some weird things during my time as a secret agent, but there has always been a rational explanation behind everything. I know for a fact that scarecrows can't talk, which meant I needed to have a serious conversation with this one!

I decided to grab my rucksack first, because I still didn't know who or what I was dealing with and might need a gadget to get me out of a sticky situation, *or* something heavy to swing at the nasty birds!

Unfortunately, Mum was lying on one of the straps of my rucksack

and when I tugged it free her book slipped down her face and her eyes popped open. She was still half-asleep and gazed up at me though sleepy eyes.

'Afternoon, Ma'am,' I said quickly, tipping my hat politely. 'I'm just off to scare some crows,' I added cheerily, prodding my fat straw belly.

Then I hurried away doing a silly
scarecrow walk.

My mum always takes ages to
wake up in the morning, so I hoped
my bizarre behaviour would make her
think she was dreaming. I whipped
out my mirror on a stick gadget and
held it up to look behind me, and saw
Mum frown for a moment and then
fall back to sleep again.

PHEW!

By the time I got back
to the talking scarecrow
I was pretty annoyed.

'Now listen
here!' I snapped,
waving a
finger at him.

'I know that scarecrows can't talk, or nod their heads, or send their nasty little birds after a young girl who is just trying to protect her picnic . . . '

'Really?' interrupted the scarecrow.

'Yes, *really*!' I said, dumping my rucksack in the grass.

'Then why are you having a conversation with one?' The scarecrow chuckled.

'Because there's something else going on here and I'm going to get to the bottom of it!' I said, rolling up my sleeves and taking a step forward.

'You picked the wrong picnic this time, Mister!'

'What are you doing?' gasped the scarecrow. 'Get away from me!'

I ignored the scarecrow's protests and began tugging at his legs, practically swinging on them to loosen the waist knot. Eventually I managed to pull them free and they landed with a soft thud on the grass, then I picked up the trousers and shook them upside down.

'Oi!'

said the
scarecrow.

'Those are
my legs!'
    'Hmmm?'
I said, picking
through the
straw to find a few curly sandwiches.

Next I grabbed the hem of his
shirt and pulled hard with my foot
propped against the vertical post for
leverage. The horizontal post ran
through the sleeves and it took all
my strength to rip it.

'Stop that!' yelled the scarecrow. 'I'm already legless, leave me my body!'

'It's not your *body*,' I grunted, straining with the effort. 'It's just rags and straw, and stolen food!' I added, and eventually the torso tumbled down and landed at my feet. When I popped open the shirt buttons I found a squished fruitcake and an apple pie among the straw.

'Now what have you got to say for yourself?' I said, pointing at the food.

The head leaned forward and peered down at the evidence.

'I have to admit, it doesn't look good,' it said.

'Oh, I haven't finished yet,' I said, rummaging in my rucksack.

I pulled out my extendable grabber-hand gadget, and waved it at what was left of the scarecrow. The head had been pretty chatty all the time it thought it was out of my reach, but now it simply quivered on its post.

'Anything to say before I pull
your head off?' I said, extending the
hand and knocking its hat off. Then I
closed the hand over the head sack of
the scarecrow. 'Any last words?'

'Who's a pretty boy then?' said
the scarecrow, as I pulled its head off.

I have to admit, I was a bit
worried about what I might find
under the sack, but when I peered

up to find a brightly
coloured parrot
perched on the post,
I was more confused than
anything else.

'You're a parrot!' I
gasped.

'Polly's the name,'
it said, bobbing its *real* head. 'Pleased
to meet you.'

I was about to quiz the
parrot when I became aware of
the crows cawing overhead.
They seemed very cross
and began dropping
in a familiar dive-bomb
display. But this time Polly
hadn't whistled a signal.

'UH OH!' said the
parrot, looking up nervously.

'Call them off!' I yelled,
grabbing my rucksack ready to fend
off the beaks.

'They won't listen to me now
they've seen I'm a just bird,' squawked
Polly. 'That's why I hid inside the
scarecrow. And now they know I
tricked them, I think they want all
the food for themselves.'

CAW! CAW! CAW!

As black birds swooped down, the frightened parrot fluttered onto my shoulder and I realised how small he was. I couldn't leave Polly to the nasty crows, so I began whirling my rucksack over my head and legged it across the field.

A few of the birds followed us, giving warning caws, but they soon rejoined the rest of the flock squabbling over the fallen food.

Away from the pecking beaks, the parrot thanked me for rescuing him.

And while I redressed
the scarecrow whose
clothes I'd borrowed,
he told me the story
of how he ended up
inside a scarecrow's
head, training
crows to steal
food for him.

Polly's owner was a university
professor who had taught him loads
of clever words to say, and quickly
discovered that his parrot was much
smarter than the average bird. Polly
said he liked living with the professor
because he wasn't kept in a cage and
could fly around freely, but one day
he'd flown too far and couldn't find
his way home again.

'I thought birds
were really good
at finding
their way
home?' I
said.

'I'm not a
homing pigeon,'
said Polly. 'But I do know my address.'

'Then couldn't you just ask
someone for directions?' I suggested.

'The professor told me not to
talk to strangers,' said the parrot. 'He
said that people wouldn't expect a
bird to be smart enough to hold a
conversation, and that I might end up
in the wrong hands.'

'Yeah,' I said. 'He's probably
right about that.'

'I could ask *you* for directions!' said the parrot, excitedly.

'I'm not sure how I would explain it to my mum though . . . ' I said, looking over at the tree. It was then that I noticed Mum had woken up and was waving at me to come and have lunch. 'Hang on a minute,' I said, pulling out the paper and my pointy pencil.

'ARRRGH!'

squawked the parrot.

'I'm not going to jab you,' I laughed. 'Give me your address . . . '

Luckily Mum bought the story about finding the parrot with a note tied to his leg, and said we'd look the address up on the map and drive him home after lunch. Then, as she unpacked the picnic, Mum told me all about the strange scarecrow dream she'd had.

'A talking scarecrow!' she chuckled. 'Can you imagine?'

'Hmmm . . .' I said, peering over my sunglasses at a guilty looking Polly.

Mum laid out the sandwiches and cake, and then frowned at the parrot perched on the edge of the picnic basket. 'Do you think it would be OK to feed him?' she asked, pulling off a piece of cake.

Polly was gazing at the lump of cake and I could tell he really wanted to say 'YES PLEASE!' But I'd warned him not to speak in front of Mum, just in case she got freaked out.

'I think he'd like that,' I smiled.

The Case of the Gobbledygook Books

I often go to the school library during lunchtime and have my sandwiches with Mrs Young, the librarian. Mrs Young is really nice and keeps books aside for me that have anything to do with secret agents. At the moment I'm into a series called *Suzy Spy*, about a secret agent who travels the world fighting crime and gets to use brilliant gadgets that the government make for her.

This particular lunchtime I went to the library hoping to get the latest *Suzy Spy* book called *Peril in Paris!* The librarian had said it was due to come in on Monday morning and that she would happily put it aside for me.

When I entered the library, Mrs Young was nowhere to be seen and standing behind her counter was a large woman with square glasses and a harsh fringe.

I'm always suspicious when a new staff member joins the school, because you never know when or where someone might try to take over the world, so I approached with caution and tipped my sunglasses.

'Where's the librarian?' I asked.

'If you're referring to the timid little bookworm that *used* to work here, she's retired!' said the woman, typing frantically on her laptop. 'You'll be dealing with me from now on. My name is Mrs Rogue.'

My secret agent senses immediately kicked in.

First of all Mrs Young was much too *young* to retire, and even if she had, she would definitely have said goodbye to me before leaving. Then there was the new librarian's ridiculous name! Evil geniuses and criminal masterminds often change their names to make them sound more villainous, and Mrs *Rogue* was the worst made-up name I'd ever heard.

It was then that I noticed the
sound of Mrs Rogue's typing was
echoed through the library and when
I looked around I saw the reading
tables where all bunched together
and had brand new laptops on them.

The laptops were identical to the one
she was using, and the kids sitting at
the keyboards were all typing at the
same lightning speed.

I casually slid along the counter
and leaned forward to get a look at
Mrs Rogue's screen, but before I could
see what she was typing, she slammed
the thing shut and glared at me.

'Is there something I can help
you with?' she snapped, drumming
her fingers impatiently on the laptop
top. 'As you can see I'm very busy,
er . . . networking all the new library
computers.'

Being a
secret agent
I'm used to
dealing with
dodgy characters,
and I was sure
Mrs Rogue was doing
more than just linking
a few laptops. But I
couldn't let her know I was onto her,
so I uttered the first thing that
came into my head.

'Suzy Spy!'
I said.

'Excuse
me?'
said the
librarian.

'The new *Suzy Spy* book,' I explained. 'Mrs Young said she'd put it aside for me.'

'Oh, I'm afraid that one has already been lent out,' said Mrs Rogue. 'A delightful young girl took it this morning. She said she already has the whole collection at home, but didn't want to crease their spines . . . '

With this the library doors swung open and Trudy Hart entered, her face buried in *Peril In Paris!* I should have known my arch nemesis had nabbed the book, but the word 'delightful' had thrown me. Trudy knows how much I love the *Suzy Spy* books, so I was fully expecting her gloat about getting the new one first.

As Trudy walked past she paused for a moment and frowned as though she didn't know who I was, then she smiled pleasantly and sat at one of the new computers. The Trudy Hart I know *never* passes up an opportunity to gloat, which meant something *seriously* dodgy was going on . . .

'Would you like to read this one instead?' the librarian said suddenly, holding up a book called *Poochie Power!*

She was wearing a smile that looked very uncomfortable on her face. 'It's about a doggie with magical powers, it's *very* funny.'

'No thanks, I think I'll look for something else,' I said, strolling away and heading for the book shelves behind Trudy Hart. I pretended to browse the books until the librarian reopened her laptop and resumed her frantic typing – then I peered over Trudy's shoulder.

Trudy had placed the book beside her and was tapping away on the keyboard along with all the other kids – her fingers a blur of manic movement! But when I looked at the screen I saw that she was typing gobbledygook!

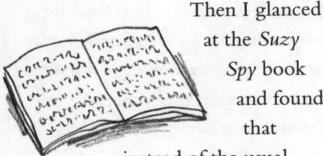

Then I glanced at the *Suzy Spy* book and found that instead of the usual opening chapter that always begins with the words 'Hi! My name is Suzy Spy . . . ' the page was also filled with gobbledygook!

Even glancing at the page made me feel a bit odd, which meant

the gobbledygook obviously wasn't gobbledygook at all. What looked like nonsense to me was probably responsible for turning Trudy into a human robot – which was *actually* a bit of an improvement!

A quick squint at the other kids' books confirmed that their pages had also been swapped for the mysterious language, and they were typing the exact same thing on their laptops, fingers jabbing at the keys like little pistons.

Then I suddenly realised where
I had seen this kind of writing before!

It was a few weeks before in
tech class. My computer had crashed
and loads of random letters and
numbers and symbols had appeared on
the screen. I'd asked the tech teacher
what this was and he explained that
it was a special language that told
computers what to do.

The kids around the tables had all been reading the same gobbledygook in their books and were acting like rapid typing robots, which *had* to mean they were being told what to do in computer language.

I peered over my sunglasses and noticed that Mrs Rogue was looking over her laptop at me. She was obviously getting suspicious, so I had to find a way to blend in with the weird robot kids.

I
pulled a
couple of
books from
the shelf
and checked
the pages. They
all had regular words in them, which
meant the librarian was handing out
the gobbledygook books herself. Like
the one she had offered me . . .

I strolled back to the counter
and smiled sweetly.

'Um, I can't find anything
interesting so I'd like to read the book
about the magic doggie, please,' I said,
hoping Mrs Rogue was keen to add
another soldier to her creepy robot
army.

The librarian grinned from ear
to ear as she passed me the book.

A quick glance inside confirmed that *Poochie Power!* was another of Mrs Rogue's gobbledygook books, so I took it to a chair tucked away behind a bookshelf. I wasn't sure how long the brain programming was supposed to take, so I waited five minutes and then wandered out again like a robot.

I sat down at one of the empty laptops, stared straight ahead and began tapping randomly at the keys as fast as I could. Then, keeping

my head still, I glanced sideways to see a very smug looking librarian peeping over the counter.

I'd obviously fooled her, and now I had to work out exactly what she was up to.

I slipped a hand down to the mouse and clicked around the desktop until I found a folder called 'TOP SECRET'. And when I opened the folder I found a document called 'My Fiendish Plan.'

'That's original!' I mumbled, clicking the file open.

 I've foiled loads
of plans to take
over the world
before, but this
lunatic librarian
was planning
to take over the
World Wide Web!
This didn't tell me what she planned
to do if she succeeded, but businesses
use the internet and loads of people
have it at home – so she'd probably be
able to access anything she wanted!

Mrs Rogue suddenly left
her counter and marched towards
the reading tables where I was still
snooping and everyone else was typing.
I quickly got rid of the folder and
resumed the random prodding of keys.

'Someone here is typing gobbledygook!' she yelled, banging her fist on the table. The sudden bang made me jump, which was a huge mistake. None of the other kids even reacted to the noise and Mrs Rogue now knew I was faking.

The librarian lurched forward and made a grab for me, but I managed to duck under the table and escape through Trudy Hart's legs.

I jumped up at the other side of the table to find Mrs Rogue tapping at my laptop, deleting what I'd typed. This proved that the robot kids were *not* just jabbing keys at random, which *had* to mean they were turbo-typing the code that would allow Mrs Rogue to take over the internet!

'You're not going to get away with this!' I said, waving a finger across the table.

'And who's going to stop me?' said the librarian, snapping the laptop shut.

'Me!' I said confidently, although I still had no idea how.

As Mrs Rogue chased me around the tables, I pressed 'DELETE' on all of the other kids' computers, hoping it might undo their programming or something like that.

But it had no effect at all and they just continued to type.

The librarian was starting to gain on me so I broke away and charged across the library, ducking down the aisles of books that were a bit narrow for someone as big as my pursuer – which at least slowed her down a bit.

But wherever I went Mrs Rogue was
still behind me, until I spotted the
store cupboard up ahead and sprinted
for it.

Luckily the door wasn't locked
and I managed to barge inside and
slam the door shut before she caught
me. I slipped the bolt into place and
peeped through the blind. Mrs Rogue

was stomping her massive feet and cursing my escape, but then I became aware of another voice coming from *inside* the room!

'Mmmf mmf fmm!' it went, which was pretty creepy.

I turned around very slowly to find Mrs Young sitting in the middle of the room! The *real* librarian was tied to a chair and had a date-stamp sticker stuck over her mouth, so I hurried forward and whipped it off quickly like a plaster.

'Amelia!' gasped Mrs Young. 'Oh, thank goodness!'

'Are you OK, Mrs Young?' I asked, and quickly set about releasing her from the ropes. 'I'm guessing you already know a madwoman has taken over the library! What happened?'

'I came in early this morning to unpack the new delivery of books,' she explained. 'And as soon as I stepped through the door a large woman with a harsh fringe pounced on me and tied me up. Then she bundled me in here!'

'Did she say anything?' I asked, undoing the last of the knots.

'Well, she did seem very cross that there were so many books. Which I thought was odd as this is a library, after all,' said Mrs Young, rubbing her wrists. 'In fact she spent the whole time ranting about how useless books were . . . '

'Evil geniuses and criminal masterminds do love to rant,' I said, stepping back over to the door.

Through the blind I could see Mrs Rogue had returned to the laptop at the counter and was typing even more furiously than before.

'Evil geniuses and criminal masterminds?' frowned Mrs Young.

'Er, yes . . . ' I said, suddenly realising I'd said too much.

I couldn't let the librarian know I was a secret agent because then it wouldn't be secret anymore. 'I mean they always love to rant in the *Suzy Spy* books.'

'Of course,' said Mrs Young, joining me at the door and looking through the blind. 'Perhaps she really *is* an evil genius or a criminal mastermind! I wonder what she's doing on that laptop?'

'I'm not sure, but I think she's trying to take over the internet,' I said, trying to sound vague and clueless. 'She also tampered with the books to make the kids write her computer code . . .'

'Tampered with my books!'
gasped Mrs Young.

I was wondering how I could
stop the fake librarian *and* keep
the real librarian safe – all without
revealing my secret agent identity,
when Mrs Young suddenly slipped the
bolt back and charged into the library!

Uh Oh!

I ran after the librarian who was
heading straight for Mrs Rogue!

'Stop what you're doing and leave my library right now!' demanded Mrs Young.

The fake librarian narrowed her eyes at the real librarian and then laughed. It was a loud booming laugh that I've heard loads of times before. The lunatic laugh of someone who thinks their plan for world domination is unstoppable.

I stood next to Mrs Young and decided to speed things along a bit.

'So what *are* you trying to do anyway?' I sighed, knowing that evil geniuses and criminal masterminds simply can't resist bragging about how clever they are. 'Aside from taking over the internet, of course!'

'I plan to rid the world of books!' said Mrs Rogue, flinging her arms in the air dramatically. 'And when I've closed down every library and bookshop and publisher, I will then be able to control what everyone reads on the internet!'

Mrs Young gasped and I scratched my head.

'What have you got against books?' I asked, stalling for time while I worked out what to do next.

'They are dusty and outdated and the people who read them are weak and dull!' growled Mrs Rogue. 'We live in an age of the information superhighway! With megabits and gigabits and downloads and upgrades . . . '

Mrs Rogue lost the thread of her rant for a moment because she had suddenly lost half of her audience. Mrs Young had hurried away and seemed  to be hiding behind one of the bookshelves.

'And that's the perfect example!' sneered Mrs Rogue, gesturing to the empty spot where Mrs Young had been standing. 'Surrounding herself with all these dusty books has turned her into a timid little mouse who flees at the first sign of . . . '

Mrs Young suddenly reappeared with a large book that she was casually flicking through. Mrs Rogue looked completely baffled as the librarian approached the counter and I was quite intrigued too.

'This is the complete works of William Shakespeare!' Mrs Young stated proudly. 'Probably the greatest writer in the history of the world!' she added, lifting the open book in preparation for a reading.

Mrs Rogue was about to stifle an exaggerated yawn when Mrs Young suddenly raised the book higher, snapped it shut and brought the massive volume down on the laptop with an almighty

BANG!

Rogue's yawn quickly became a scream as the keys and wires and other broken bits pinged out of her laptop and showered around her. Then a puff of black smoke rose from the crushed computer.

Rogue's defeated scream was followed by a moment of silence, which included the absence of key tapping from the kids on the reading tables. They were all frowning, except for Trudy who was glaring, which meant the smashed computer had broken the spell. Then they turned to the source of the scream with fingers pressed to their lips.

'*SHHHHHHHH!*' they all hissed together.

Mrs Rogue looked startled for

SHHHHHHHH!

a moment and then fixed her sights on Mrs Young. Suddenly the large lunatic vaulted over the counter and chased the librarian into the store cupboard where the door slammed shut behind them.

UH OH! I thought, as the sounds of banging and crashing echoed through the library. Moments later the door swung open and Mrs Rogue was tied to the chair with an 'EX LIBRARY' sticker on her mouth!

'But how . . .' I gasped, as Mrs
Young left the room dusting off her
hands.

'I read the *Suzy Spy* books
too,' smiled the librarian. 'Do you
remember what happened in *Menace
in Milan*?'

'It's one of my favourites,' I said,
recalling how Suzy circled the crook
with a rope like a cattle rancher
and lassoed him to an office chair.

Which was obviously how the nimble librarian had overpowered Mrs Rogue.

'Speaking of which . . . ' said Mrs Young.

The librarian went behind the counter and pulled out a brand new copy of *Peril in Paris!* She handed it to me with a smile and then quickly gathered up the gobbledygook books from the tables.

Trudy was about to protest
when Mrs Young took *her* book, and
then decided against it. I think she
went off the *Suzy Spy* books that day.

When the police came to take Mrs Rogue away, they applauded Mrs Young for her extraordinary skill and bravery in defeating the criminal – and the librarian laughed and said she felt like a real secret agent!

Then I sat down with my sandwiches and started reading the latest *Suzy Spy* book.

I was really looking forward to finding out what she'd get up to in Paris, because sometimes it's really nice to let someone else save the world for a change.

AGENT Amelia Ghost Diamond!

A jewel with a world-dominating spirit; a plague of furry cat burglars; and a criminal mastermind with a creepy weed army. Agent Amelia just has to get busy to save the world!

AGENT AMELIA: Ghost Diamond! ISBN 9781842706626 £4.99

Zombie COWS!

Clockwork farm animals,
a modern day Pied Piper and
a case of exploding cakes:
Agent Amelia has a lot on
her plate as she fights to
save the world!

AGENT AMELIA: Zombie Cows! ISBN 9781842706633 £4.99

AGENT Amelia — Hypno Hounds!

A deserted village haunted by handbag hounds; a mad science teacher hiding experimental pompom creatures; and some thieving roller skating teddies. It's enough to keep Amelia active, saving the world!

AGENT AMELIA: Hypno Hounds! ISBN 9781842708163 £4.99